Science Matters
STORMS

Christine Webster

WEIGL PUBLISHERS INC.

Published by Weigl Publishers Inc.
350 5th Avenue, Suite 3304, PMB 6G
New York, NY USA 10118-0069
Website: www.weigl.com
Copyright © 2007 WEIGL PUBLISHERS INC.

Library of Congress Cataloging-in-Publication Data

Webster, Christine.
  Storms / by Christine Webster.
      p. cm. -- (Science matters)
  Includes bibliographical references and index.
  ISBN 1-59036-412-0 (alk. paper) -- ISBN 1-59036-418-X (pbk. : alk. paper)
  1. Storms--Juvenile literature. I. Title. II. Series.
  QC941.3.W43 2007
  551.55--dc22
                                    2005029919

Printed in China
2 3 4 5 6 7 8 9 0 10 09 08 07 06

Editor Frances Purslow
Design and Layout Terry Paulhus

Cover: Violent storms often gather strength over water.

Photograph Credits
University of Heidelberg, ESA: page 12T; **NASA,ESA, M. Robberto (Space Telescope Science Institute/ESA) and the Hubble Space Telescope Orion Treasury Project Team plus C.R. O'Dell (Rice University), and NASA**: pages 12 & 13 background; **NASA, ESA, J. Hester and A. Loll (Arizona State University)**: page 14L; **Warren Faidley/Weatherstock.com**: page 19.

Contents

Studying Storms 4

How Storms Form 6

Thunderstorms 8

Tornadoes 10

Sky Technology 12

Hurricanes 14

Blizzards 16

Storm Chaos 18

Surfing Storm Science 20

Science in Action 21

What Have You Learned? 22

Words to Know/Index 24

Studying Storms

A picture from space may show Earth looking calm, with quiet, blue oceans and white, fluffy clouds. Other days, it may show swirling masses of dark cloud bringing wind, rain, or snow. Earth's atmosphere is always moving and changing. The atmosphere is a layer of air that surrounds the planet. Huge battles take place there every day. Masses of cold air and warm air ram into each other. Winds blow and storms form.

There are many kinds of storms. **Hurricanes**, **blizzards**, and **tornadoes** are just some of the storms that occur on Earth.

■ Storms are violent changes in the atmosphere. Storm formation can be seen from space.

Storm Facts

Did you know that frogs and fish have been known to fall to Earth inside **hailstones**? Keep reading to learn more interesting facts about stormy weather.

- A lightning bolt contains enough electricity to power an average household for two weeks.

- Hurricanes, blizzards, and tornadoes contain large amounts of energy. They can cause damage and loss of life.

- The highest waterspout ever seen was almost a mile (1.6 kilometers) high.

- The United States averages 800 tornadoes per year. That is more than any other country in the world.

How Storms Form

All storms have two things in common. They have low air pressure in their center, and they have wind. These conditions occur because of uneven heating on Earth.

As the Sun heats Earth, some areas receive more of the Sun's heat than others. This uneven heating causes areas of low pressure and high pressure. Winds blow from high pressure areas to low pressure areas. Winds blowing from all sides into a low pressure area create a storm.

● Storms usually produce rain, ice, or snow.

Storm Myths

Long ago, people did not know why storms happened. They told stories or myths about storms.

Some ancient peoples believed that thunder and lightning were weapons thrown to Earth by angry gods. The Ancient Greeks believed that lightning was caused by a god named Zeus.

In Scandinavia, it was believed that thunder came from a god named Thor. The rumbling sound was Thor riding his cart over the clouds.

Zeus

Ancient Romans believed in a god named Neptune. He was the god of the sea. They believed that storms at sea were caused by Neptune's quick temper.

Tornadoes

A tornado is sometimes called a twister. It is a twisting black funnel of cloud and air that spins downward. If fast-moving cold air high in the sky crosses over slow-moving warm air near the ground, the air begins to swirl. The funnel creates a vacuum that sucks up warm air from below. The funnel stretches and grows downward until it touches the ground. Then it lifts up again.

Tornado winds are the strongest winds on Earth. They can blow more than 250 miles (400 km) per hour. Tornados can blow apart buildings and throw cars through the air.

■ A tornado in Pampa, Texas, reached speeds up to 300 miles (480 km) per hour.

Waterspouts

Waterspouts are tornadoes that form over water. Like tornadoes, rising air currents suck warm air from below. In the case of waterspouts, the funnel is made of a thin cloud of water droplets.

Waterspouts are most common in warm, moist areas, such as the Florida Keys. Although they are often smaller and weaker than tornadoes, which occur on land, waterspouts are still dangerous. They can overturn boats or threaten swimmers. Winds in waterspouts can be as fast as 190 miles (300 km) per hour.

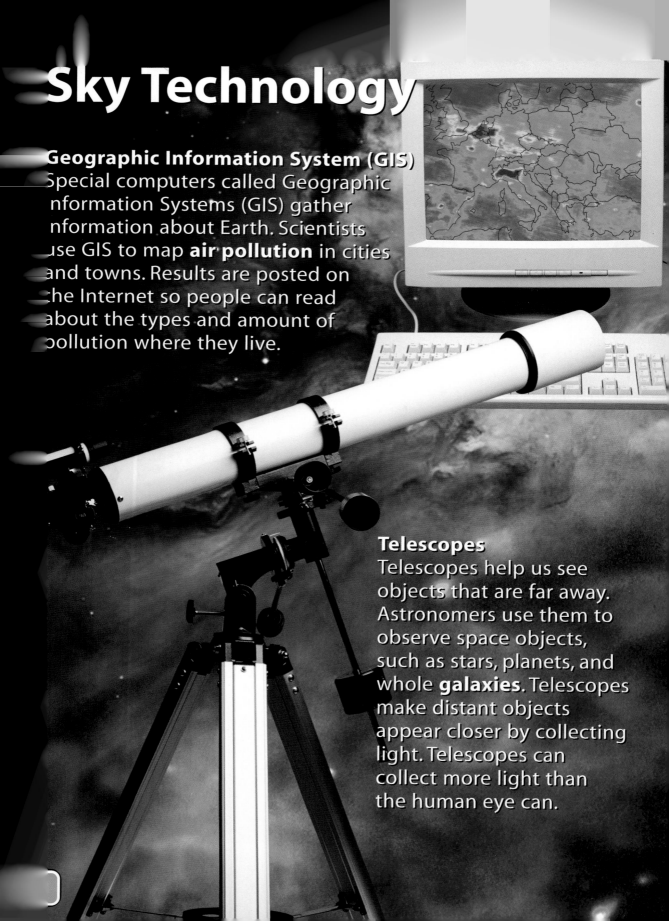

Sky Technology

Geographic Information System (GIS)

Special computers called Geographic Information Systems (GIS) gather information about Earth. Scientists use GIS to map **air pollution** in cities and towns. Results are posted on the Internet so people can read about the types and amount of pollution where they live.

Telescopes

Telescopes help us see objects that are far away. Astronomers use them to observe space objects, such as stars, planets, and whole **galaxies**. Telescopes make distant objects appear closer by collecting light. Telescopes can collect more light than the human eye can.

Weather Satellite

Weather satellites are spacecraft that circle Earth. They provide a weather watch on the entire planet. Weather satellites take photographs of Earth's atmosphere. These help meteorologists predict storms and other weather patterns. These satellites also carry special instruments that record information on computers. They monitor events in the atmosphere, such as auroras, dust storms, pollution, and cloud systems.

Radar

Meteorologists gather huge amounts of information in order to predict the weather. **Radar** can tell them what is inside a cloud. This can be rain or hail. Radar can also track a storm that is coming. It helps meteorologists warn people if the storm is dangerous.

Hurricanes

Hurricanes are the biggest storms on Earth. They can stretch 300 miles (480 km) across. A hurricane is a large storm shaped like a donut. It brings heavy rains and strong winds that blow around a calm center. The center is called the eye of the storm.

A hurricane forms over a **tropical** sea. Warm, moist air rises upward, sucking in air continuously. The air then begins to spiral inward toward the eye. If winds reach 74 miles (119 km) per hour, the storm is called a hurricane. Hurricanes are also known as typhoons or cyclones. Their high winds and huge waves cause immense damage on land. As a hurricane travels inland, it loses strength.

■ Hurricane Katrina caused 1,053 deaths in the New Orleans area in 2005.

Storm Alert

Violent storms are hard to predict more than a day in advance. Some form in less than an hour. The government warns people via radio or television about when and where a bad storm is likely to hit.

A weather advisory alerts people about a severe storm that might be on the way. It is too early to know for certain.

A weather watch warns people that a bad storm could develop very soon. People should watch the sky and listen for updated **forecasts**.

A weather warning tells that dangerous weather is happening right now. Take cover right away.

■ Hurricane Isabel was tracked by meteorologists at the National Hurricane Center in Miami.

Blizzards

Blizzards are winter storms that bring extreme cold, high winds, and heavy snowfall. Blizzards are formed when air pressure, temperature, and moisture change. To be called a blizzard, winds must be at least 32 miles (50 km) per hour. Also, **visibility** must be limited to 500 feet (150 m). High winds can form snowdrifts that block roads. People can be without heat, electricity, or transportation. Forceful winds and very cold temperatures can make it dangerous to be outside. Skin that is not covered can quickly freeze in a blizzard.

■ A blizzard can bring an entire city to a standstill.

Storms on Other Planets

Earth is not the only planet to have severe storms. Saturn, Neptune, Uranus, Mars, and Jupiter also experience violent weather.

Neptune and Saturn have very strong winds. They blow up to 700 miles (1,130 km) per hour.

On Jupiter, lightning bolts light up the sky. The Great Red Spot seen on Jupiter's surface is actually a large storm that has continued for more than 300 years.

Uranus also has powerful storms. They usually occur in spring.

Fierce dust storms are common on Mars. These dust storms can last for months. They are so strong that they can spin into tornado-like twisters.

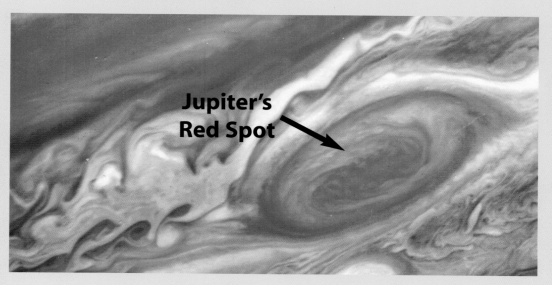

Jupiter's Red Spot

Storm Chaos

Some storms cause great damage. Tornadoes can destroy anything in their path. A tornado's strong suction is able to suck up and toss around trees, buildings, and even people. Thunderstorms sometimes cause **flash floods**. Lightning strikes trees, which may cause fires. When hurricanes blow in from the ocean, heavy winds and large waves rip apart towns along the coast. The rain that accompanies hurricanes may flood cities and farmland. If a winter blizzard drops many feet of snow on the ground, people stay home for days. An **ice storm** can snap power lines, leaving people without heat and light during cold weather.

■ Flooding is the most common natural disaster. It can be caused by various types of storms.

Storm Chaser

A storm chaser is a person who chases storms. Storm chasers try to get as close to storms as possible.

They watch how the storm behaves and use special equipment to make measurements. Modern storm chasers use computers, **anemometers**, radar, cameras, and portable weather stations. This equipment takes pictures and readings from the storm, such as air pressure, wind speed and direction. Meteorologists use this information to help them predict the path of fierce storms, such as tornadoes.

Surfing Storm Science

How can I find more information about storms?
- Libraries have many interesting books about storms.
- The Internet has some excellent websites dedicated to storms
- A meteorologist can provide information about storms.

Where can I find a good website to learn more about storms?
National Center for Atmospheric Research
http://eo.ucar.edu/webweather
- Click on the various links to learn about different types of weather. This website includes fun activities as well.

How can I find out more about storms?
Storm Predictions Center
www.spc.noaa.gov
- Look for any weather watches, warnings, or advisories by clicking anywhere on the map.

Science in Action

Make Your Own Tornado

Create a mini-tornado.

You will need:

- water
- a 250-milliliter (8-ounce) jar with lid
- a teaspoon
- vinegar
- clear, liquid dish soap
- glitter

Add water to the jar until it is almost full.

Add a spoonful of vinegar.

Add a spoonful of dish soap.

Add a sprinkle or two of glitter.

Tightly close the lid and spin the jar.

What happened to the glitter as you spun the jar? Did all of the glitter move at the same speed? What happens when you stop spinning the jar?

What Have You Learned?

1. What is the atmosphere?

2. What is a violent change in the atmosphere called?

3. What is the most dangerous thunderstorm called?

4. Name three characteristics of a typical storm.

5. What type of storm has a funnel cloud?

6 What type of storm has an "eye"?

7 Why do you see lightning and then hear thunder later?

8 What is a blizzard?

9 Name the biggest storm on Earth.

10 What type of storm has the fastest winds?

Words to Know

air pollution: harmful materials, such as chemicals and gas, that make air dirty

anemometer: an instrument for measuring wind

blizzards: winter storms with cold winds and blowing snow

downdraft: wind or air that is pushed downwards

flash floods: floods with rapidly rising water

forecasts: predictions

galaxies: large groups of stars

hailstones: pieces of ice that fall during a thunderstorm

hurricanes: very strong windstorms that build over the ocean

ice storm: a storm that coats everything in a layer of ice

radar: a system that uses radio waves to locate objects

tornadoes: twisting black funnels of cloud and air

tropical: regions near the equator with hot, humid climate

visibility: the ability to see, based on weather conditions

Index

air pressure 6, 16, 19
atmosphere 4, 13

cyclone 14

hail 5, 8, 9

lightning 5, 7, 8, 17, 18

meteorology 13
myth 7

snow 4, 6, 16, 18
supercell 8

thunder 7, 8
twister 10
typhoon 14

waterspout 5, 11
weather 13, 15, 20
wind 4, 6, 8, 10, 14, 16, 17, 18, 19